WHY DOES THE MOUNTAIN CRY?

NEHA SHETTIYAR

Made with ♥ on the Notion Press Platform
www.notionpress.com

For all the wonderful readers.

I hope you enjoy reading these simple and short stories.

This book is dedicated to my daughter, Tanishka.

Contents

ONE

WHY DOES THE MOUNTAIN CRY?

This was not the first time the department had asked Pranjali to hold discussions about a rural development project. She frequently received requests to visit remote areas and help the local people understand the importance of development for their communities, enabling them to connect better with the outside world. The government was introducing numerous schemes aimed at uplifting rural and geographically isolated regions. Key components of these projects included the construction of schools, housing, roads, hospitals, and more. To lay the foundation for these initiatives, it was essential to communicate with the local population and secure their agreement to avoid any obstacles later on. Pranjali, known for her skill in conducting diplomatic talks, had always executed this task flawlessly. However, this time she felt uneasy about the new assignment because it involved the only place on earth that she had been avoiding. Reluctant to participate in the project, she attempted to excuse herself, but the Chief was adamant. He insisted that Pranjali visit 'Sampanpur.'

Sampanpur was a hidden gem on Earth, bordered by the sea on one side and a mountain on the other. The only way to reach this place was by sea, as the massive mountain, Devshaila, stood between Sampanpur and the rest of the world. Recognizing the breathtaking natural beauty of Sampanpur, the government devised a plan to develop it for tourism. Several attempts were made to cut through the mountain and construct a connecting road, but progress halted due to resistance from the villagers, who staged protests. When authorities forcefully tried to access the mountain, they encountered an inexplicable phenomenon that many reported as strange paranormal activities. Finding no alternative, the authorities concluded that only someone who understands the people of Sampanpur could address this challenging situation. After scanning the database, it was revealed that Pranjali hails from Sampanpur so she was assigned the task to hold talks with villagers and to jump start the project.

After scanning the database, it was revealed that Pranjali is from Sampanpur, and she was assigned the task of engaging with the villagers to jumpstart the project. For years, Pranjali had been trying to distance herself and her family from Sampanpur. This morning, when she was unexpectedly pulled into a meeting and handed the assignment for Sampanpur, memories of her past in that place flooded her mind. She wasn't even consulted about her interest in visiting her ancestral land. Instead, the Chief assumed she would be eager to go back and simply handed her the official documents and assignment letter. Feeling anxious and annoyed, Pranjali went to the window for some fresh air. She pulled out her mobile phone and dialed Rishi's number.

"This time, I am asked to go to Sampanpur for the project," she said in a distress tone without any greetings.

"Where?... Sampanpur? Why?... No! I mean... Pranjali, listen to me. Please don't accept this assignment," unable to grab words, Rishi stammered.

The news came as a shock to him. He knew how much Pranjali disliked Sampanpur. He was reminded of their college days when Pranjali would often cry because people teased her and called her "Junglee." She was emotionally devastated during that time, feeling belittled and inferior. It was only thanks to Rishi that she was able to overcome these challenges. He stood by her side and supported her throughout. After finishing college, they got married and moved to a better city. With Rishi's encouragement, Pranjali was able to leave her past behind and worked hard to build a successful career. She earned the respect she had always craved, both at work and in society.

Rishi never wanted Pranjali to return to the Sampanpur mess. He had heard many stories about that place. If it hadn't been for Pranjali's mother, she might have suffered the same fate as many other children had.

"I tried talking to the Chief but it's not working," Pranjali replied, biting her nails.

Just then an office staff approached her and she had to cut the conversation with Rishi.

"I am needed in the meeting room. Catch you later. Bye!"

"Alright..., don't worry. We will figure out something. You just relax. Bye! take care!" he hurriedly said as the call ended.

Although the conversation was brief, it made her feel better. Rishi was a strong pillar of support in her life, and sharing her problems with him always provided her relief. In the evening, both Rishi and Pranjali wanted to discuss

Sampanpur, but they avoided bringing it up in front of their teenage daughter, Mrunal, who was unaware of the situation. After dinner, when Mrunal went to her room, Pranjali thought it was a better time to talk.

In a subdued tone, she said, "I can't deal with the people in Sampanpur. They haven't changed at all. I heard a lot about them this morning. The department has already made a futile attempt, and now they want me to join them. Those people are so conservative and primitive. They won't allow Sampanpur to develop. They are superstitious and will never accept any change. They still want to dwell in the Stone Age." Pranjali was frustrated.

"Please don't bother yourself. Try to convince the Chief that your visit shall surely be unfruitful." Rishi's face hardened as he spoke.

"I have already mentioned this, but he believes that my presence and words might soften the people of Sampanpur and encourage a sensible conversation. He wants me to give it a try."

"So, what have you decided?"

"Do I have a choice?"

"Just give him a rational explanation. Try talking to him and convincing him tomorrow." His words irritated Pranjali.

"Come on, Rishi... Do you really think I haven't tried to speak with him? The department isn't aware of what is happening in Sampanpur. They don't understand that the people of Sampanpur are not ordinary. The only relief is that I don't have to stay in Sampanpur. My arrangements are made in Devapur. I'll also get a chance to meet Maa; it's been a long time since I've seen her."

"Oh... I have an idea. Stay in Devapur and visit Sampanpur once. Talk to some elderly people there, prepare a report based on your findings, and return in a day or two. This way, you'll be in a win-win position."

"Brilliant! This should work. There's no point in having deep discussions with them. If I go as a government officer, they won't talk to me. It needs to be a casual visit. Let me start packing; I'll be leaving the day after tomorrow."

Finally, things were sorted for Pranjali, yet there was still a hesitation within her. The next morning, Mrunal learned that her mother was planning to visit Devapur. She had never been to her grandmother's place; it was always her grandmother who visited them. Mrunal wanted to explore village life, making her eager to accompany her mother on this trip. However, Pranjali refused to take her along. Rishi was also against it, but Mrunal was determined to go at any cost. After a long, dramatic day, Mrunal finally convinced her parents. Pranjali agreed, but only on the condition that Mrunal would stay with her grandmother and avoid wandering around alone. Mrunal eagerly accepted the first condition, but her mischievous spirit was resistant to the second. With their luggage packed, both Pranjali and Mrunal were ready for the journey.

After a long and tiresome journey, they finally reached Devapur.

Devapur was a small town with basic facilities that allowed its residents to lead simple lives. Its most notable feature was its role as a connecting hub to Sampanpur, thanks to the ferry services it offered. Although Pranjali's mother lived in Devapur, Pranjali preferred to stay at the PWD guest house. This guest house was located at the base of Mount Devshaila, which separated Devapur from Sampanpur. Ramaraju served as the caretaker of the guest house. Over the years, the guest house had barely any visitors, but recently, the number of guests had increased, keeping Ramaraju quite busy.

When Pranjali and Mrunal arrived at the guest house, Mrunal felt disappointed to learn that they would not be staying at her grandmother's house that night.

"Why aren't we going to Grandma's house?" Mrunal asked, sounding annoyed.

"It's an official tour, so I need to be here. Tomorrow morning, we'll visit Grandma's house. You can stay with her while I'm out for work. I've already informed her. Her place is not too far from here," Pranjali explained.

Dinner was served, which included chapati, rice, dal, a gravy of mixed vegetables, and for dessert, they enjoyed special kheer that Ramaraju's wife had prepared. Pranjali and Mrunal savored the simple, delicious, and piping hot meal, with Mrunal particularly enjoying the kheer. Ramaraju's wife smiled as she watched them appreciate her recipe. After a satisfying dinner, both mother and daughter went to bed. Around midnight, Mrunal woke up to the sound of someone crying. She shook her mother to wake her. Pranjali stirred awake, looking worried and surprised. She carefully stepped out of her room and called out to Ramaraju.

"Madam, please go back to your room and close the door. Please don't step out until morning. This is for your own safety," he cautioned her.

Feared with his words, she closed the door and chose to act as he said.

"What's the matter Ramaraju?" Pranjali called out from inside.

"Cries are from the mountain. They are trying to wake him up. You shall soon come to know," he replied "If you need anything please call me but please don't open the door."

As she closed the door and turned around, her eyes were drawn to the windows. Gently moving the curtains aside, she found the mountain right in front of her. A large fire blazed at its peak. She recognized it immediately; she had grown up hearing the stories about this mountain. In fact, she recalled having heard those cries before. Soon, however, the cries ceased, leaving Mrunal feeling terrified. Pranjali became increasingly worried about Mrunal's state. She wanted to leave this place as soon as possible.

The next day, Pranjali dropped Mrunal off at her grandmother's house. Mrunal was still shaken by the previous night's incident. Pranjali created a story, claiming that the cries came from a nearby house. Mrunal wasn't entirely convinced by the story but chose not to ask any questions. Pranjali then left to catch the ferry to Sampanpur, accompanied by Anirudha, a colleague who had made unsuccessful attempts to engage with the villagers. They waited for the ferry at the jetty. As Pranjali looked across the horizon, she reminisced about a time when she waited for a similar ferry with her father. He was the only educated person in the tribal village of Sampanpur, and everyone referred to him as 'Masterji' out of respect. Despite his education, he chose to remain in Sampanpur to serve his community. Soon, the ferry arrived. Lost in her myriad thoughts, Pranjali stepped onto the ferry without realizing it. As it cut through the water, the ferry made its way to Sampanpur, and Pranjali cherished her childhood memories along the journey.

"Ma'am, we have arrived," Anirudha said with a smile as he noticed Pranjali gazing joyfully at the sea. She felt as if someone had jolted her awake from a beautiful dream.

"Indeed! Time to move..." she sighed as the ferry came to a stop at the rustic jetty of Sampanpur.

"Memories!" Anirudha grinned at her.

"Yes, memories... good ones," she replied, smiling back at him as they stepped off the ferry. A blissful breeze enveloped her as she set foot on the land that was once her home. It felt like a warm welcome back. Pranjali had left Sampanpur at the age of twelve to make Devapur her permanent home. Her mother had kept her away from this land in hopes of securing a better future.

The tides of mixed emotions rose in her heart. She never hated this land; she simply wanted to distance herself from the primitive mindset of its people. Her mind and heart were at war. Her heart urged her to stay and understand the people of Sampanpur, who were constantly fighting against the government, while her mind insisted, she stick to her plan. In the end, her mind won the battle.

Pranjali and Anirudha went to the Panchayat office, where she met Sampat, the current Sarpanch of Sampanpur and an old friend. Upon recognizing her, he was initially happy to see her return, but his expression changed when he noticed Anirudha accompanying her. Sampat realized that Pranjali was the new government officer assigned to conduct bilateral talks regarding a developmental project. Out of respect, he asked her to clarify whether she was visiting Sampanpur as an official representative.

Pranjali undertood that Anirudha's presence made Sampat uncomfortable. To alleviate the tension, she suggested that Anirudha wait at the Panchayat office. The office itself was in a dilapidated state, having been constructed years ago by the government. The Panchayat secretary only came by occasionally, and it was rare for anyone else to visit. However, he was present today as he had been instructed to do so.

To foster a more productive dialogue, Pranjali encouraged Sampat to join her for a walk around the village. Sampat happily agreed and was overwhelmed to welcome an old friend.

As they walked through dusty lanes, Sampat said," Pranjali, after you left Sampanpur many young girls and boys followed your footsteps. You were an inspiration to them. Like your baba, some studied hard and returned home while many chose to stay away. We are now only a handful of people left who are trying to save and protect this land. The wave of development and modernization had hit us hard but we didn't give up. Together, we fought, but this time it seems to be difficult."

"I understand the situation. I may have left this place, but it is dearer to me than anywhere else in the world. It pains me to see that even though the world has changed, my people are still deprived of basic facilities. The school doesn't even have proper teachers. No teacher is willing to accept transfer to Sampanpur. For every single need, you are forced to commute to Devapur. The government is willing to provide you with good facilities, and it is your right to make use of them."

"You speak like other officers. Anyways, it is our right to make use of facilities but it is our duty to protect Devshaila and Sampanpur. Let us leave this topic here. Let me take you to my house and introduce you to my children."

Sampat's house was modest and lively. His son was preparing for the Engineering entrance exam while his daughter was a teacher. Pranjali was happy to see the children were doing so well.

"Children in Sampanpur are receiving an education and putting it to good use," he said proudly. Pranjali was impressed to learn that the children were making progress, but she was puzzled about why they opposed government facilities in Sampanpur. It seemed mysterious to her that, despite their education, the young people remained in a remote area with minimal resources.

"If people have changed, then why hasn't this place changed?" she questioned.

Sampat smiled in response. "We haven't stopped our children from progressing. I believe they have made progress, but they remain deeply rooted in this land. They understand the value of nature and know that it needs to be conserved. Unlike many others, they prioritize nature over money." He paused to gauge Pranjali's expression, wanting her to understand that no one in Sampanpur was interested in promoting or boosting tourism. "Don't you want to visit your home?" he asked, attempting to shift the subject.

"There is nothing left in that house that waits for me," she said gravely.

The house, once filled with family members, was now just an abandoned property with no one interested in claiming it. After Pranjali's father passed away, her mother took her and left Sampanpurmoving to her maternal home in Devapur. She left her mother-in-law behind, as the older woman was unwilling to leave their ancestral house. Unlike Pranjali's mother, her paternal family was very orthodox, and Pranjali's mother had never approved of their methods and beliefs, so she kept Pranjali away from them.

It was evening when Pranjali reached her mother's place, she found Mrunal laughing and enjoying her grandmother's company. After the previous night's incident, Prajanli was worried for Mrunal but watching her giggle and smile, she was relieved. Pranjali's mother insisted that she stay over for the night. Pranjali agreed to this as she had a lot to discuss with her.

At night Pranjali noted the day's details in her journal. As she revisited the details, she concluded that Sampat and people like him in the village were influencing the youth to remain trapped in the marshy lifestyle of Sampanpur. She realized that it was the need of the hour to make these young minds understand that with a better infrastructure and resources, they could build a brighter future. Pranjali felt compelled to take action to change their perspectives. Later, she shared her thoughts with her mother. However, her mother gave her no affirmative response, "They shall never change. Take your grandmother, for example; she stayed there until her last breath. They have a lot of stories to tell if you try to reason with them. They are very hard on their beliefs. The new generation is no different from the old one. It's better not to waste your time and energy on them. In fact, you should pack your bags and leave as soon as you can."

Pranjali understood her mother's concerns, but she was genuinely impressed by how well Sampat's children and other local youths were performing academically. She wanted to instigate positive change for them. She believed that proper road connectivity would open up new opportunities and lead to prosperity in the area. Furthermore, Sampanpur was blessed with natural beauty, and improving infrastructure could enhance eco-tourism, which would, in turn, create business and job opportunities for the community. Pranjali made a firm decision to stay and persuade Sampat to support the project. Although she recognized the challenges ahead, her determination remained strong.

The next morning, Pranjali met Anirudha and gathered all the details of previous meetings with the Sampanpur people. The documents indicated that none of the peaceful talks had been successful because the villagers believed the mountain was haunted and any disturbance could lead to disaster. Apart from that, Anirudha also shared a story he had heard from the locals about the mountain and its cries.

"Ma'am, what if the story is true? I mean...the villagers are so sure, even we people have heard the mountain crying." Anirudha said with hesitation as Pranjali was going through the documents.

"That's not possible. Those are nothing but rumors and fabricated stories to scare people away. There is nothing abnormal about that mountain. It's merely superstition," Pranjali quickly rejected.

Since childhood, Pranjali had always been hearing the story of the Sage who once lived on the Devshaila mountain. It was said that he helped the tribals of Sampanpur and Devapur. He would cure their illness and pain by providing them medicines and herbs. For this reason, the tribals worshipped him. It happened once that some invaders from a far away country destroyed Devapur and were about to set foot on Devshaila. The Sage went ahead to stop them but the ruthless invaders beheaded him. No sooner did the Sage breath his last, the sky thundered, the lighting struck, the sea turned furious and washed away the enemy army. The villagers who survived cried and mourned on seeing the Sage's lifeless body. This awakened his soul and forced it to stay on the mountain forever. Thereafter, any outsider who tried to disturb the peace of Mount Devshaila would face the wrath of the Sage's spirit. Mount Devshaila and Sampanpur remain under his protection and care. His spirit would haunt the enemy to death.

It was clear to Pranjali that time has come to have unwavering and hard talks with villagers. Wasting no more time, she headed to Sampanpur. Anirudha and two more officers went along with her but she asked them to wait at the Panchayat office's shed. She decided to head alone towards Sampat's house but considering the earlier encounters, the Panchayat secretary insisted on going along with her. Anirudha wasn't willing to be left behind so he followed her. Pranjali wasn't interested to get into any further discussions on petty topics so made no objections.

Sampat's son Vishwas saw Pranjali coming to their house along with the two gentlemen, this made him upset. Sampat already knew Pranjali's motive but somewhere deep in his heart he thought, she might understand him. He welcomed them home. Without a word or an eye contact with the other two guests, he spoke casually to Pranjali.

She tried to get to the topic for which she had made her visit but Sampat was smart enough to drop the subject. Pranjali was not going to give up easily. As the conversation continued, she looked at Vishwas and asked, "So Vishwas, how do you manage college and coaching? I mean do you commute daily to Devapur?"

"Yes, I do" he replied plainly.

"Wearisome!" she expressed.

This was her chance and she pounced upon the opportunity to extend the topic further. Gradually, the talks turned into arguments and finally into a heated debate. The raised voices gathered the crowd outside Sampat's house. Some of them came inside to check.

Vishwas was convinced that Pranjali was being rational, so he had no valid points to oppose her. Living on the isolated land made it very difficult for him and others to pursue higher education. Every day, they struggled to reach schools and colleges. This was the primary reason why many of his friends left Sampanpur for good.

The atmosphere got tense. Pranjali was not going to let it go easily. She was jaded hearing all those old-time stories over and over again. She wanted to do something especially for students like Vishwas who struggled day-in and day-out. Frustrated with the silly behavior of the villagers, she warned them, "The road shall be constructed if not today then tomorrow. You better not create obstacles. Just stay away."

Sampat had lost his cool, he warned her, "Try your luck Pranjali Madam. We know how to save our land."

Pranjali, Anirudha and the Panchayat secretary left Sampat's house making their way through the crowd that was gathered outside.

Pranjali declared that there can't be any further talks, now was the time to get into action. She drafted a detailed report regarding her communications with the villagers and sent it to the Chief giving him a confirmation that villagers are stubborn but the construction work can be started since it wouldn't damage anyone's personal property. Moreover, any resistance from their side could be handled through legal action.

This was a green signal that the department was waiting for. After Pranjali's email, the Chief insisted she should take the lead and actively participate in the initial phase of the project. This time, Pranjali willingly agreed.

The stay which was supposed to be for two to three days was now extended to weeks. Work kept Pranjali busy so Mrunal mostly stayed at her grandmother's house. Having ample spare time, her inquisitive mind pushed her to explore Devapur. Soon she made new friends who told her the mysterious stories of Sampanpur and Mount Devshaila. She secretly began hanging out with them in the forests of Devshaila. Those mystical stories captivated her and motivated her to dive deeper into them. Mrunal grew up in a cocoon atmosphere so hanging out with friends turned out to be adventurous and fascinating to her. One of her friends told her about her grandfather and his abandoned house in Sampanpur. She grew eager to know more about her lineage. This new friend told her that he knew everything about her family and promised to take her to that house. Her friend's name was **Vishwas.**

Mrunal's mind was filled with umpteen questions. She wondered why she hadn't been told about her ancestry. But, the most important question was,"Why does the mountain cry?" She wanted to confront her grandmother and parents but hesitated. Instead, she waited for the right time and opportunity.

She played naive in front of her mother and grandmother. Gradually, she innocently and indirectly started interrogating her grandmother. Her grandmother knew that Mrunal would come up with such questions someday as she had new friends in Devapur and would often hang out with them. Grandmother was well prepared for this day so she had prepared a simple and plain answer, "Your mother and I left Sampanpur for a better life. My in-laws weren't willing to join me. They loved the house and Sampanpur. They respected my choice and I respected theirs."

When Mrunal asked her grandmother about the story of Sage and Sampanpur, she simply said, "It's just another fictional story, much like the novel you read. Listen to it, enjoy it, and leave it."

Finally, the day had arrived. All the arrangements were complete. Pranjali, Anirudha, and the team arrived at the foot of Mount Devshaila with all the necessary equipment to carve a road. This road was intended to connect the villages of Devapur and Sampanpur. They had obtained all the required approvals from the authorities, so legally, no one could stop them. The only potential obstacle could be the villagers of Sampanpur, but Pranjali was determined to overcome any challenges. To prevent disruptions, the local police had been informed and were on their way to assist.

No sooner did the dozer hit Mount Devshaila's foot than everyone around heard loud cries. There was smoke seen on the mountain top and the boulders came tumbling down. This erupted panic and hassle among the people. Leaving the machines behind, the workers and the officers ran to safety. Soon the entire mountain was engulfed in a dense smoke.

"It's the Sage! He is angry! Run for your life!" one of the workers shouted hysterically. Hearing this, many of the workers began to flee the mountain, some stumbling in their panic. Despite the minimal visibility, Pranjali could see Anirudha running alongside the frightened workers and officers. The intensity of the cries and chaos was increasing. She felt as if the world around her was spinning. Through the dense smoke, she could make out a pair of red eyes staring at her. Gradually, darkness enveloped her vision, and she fainted.

Pranjali slowly opened her eyes and found herself in a hospital room, with her daughter Mrunal sitting by her side.

"How are you feeling, Mumma?" Mrunal asked with a warm smile.

"Better," Pranjali replied in a weak voice. Although her blood pressure had spiked, all her other reports were normal. She was fortunate to have escaped with only a few minor injuries. After a while, she inquired about the others who were present at the place of the accident. Mrunal informed her that some workers were badly injured while others had minor bruises; however, they were all deeply traumatized. The workers claimed to have seen the spirit of the Sage, furiously trying to drive them away.

The incident had shattered Pranjali. Her mind wasn't ready to believe what her eyes had witnessed- 'the pair of red eyes'. The pressure on her mind made her blood pressure fluctuate. She started feeling sleepy. Mrunal realized this, she helped Pranjali lay back on the bed. Just then her eyes fell on the prescription that was kept on the table, the nurse had asked her to get medicines. She quickly grabbed the prescription and hurried to the chemist store which was on the ground floor.

'Knock' **'Knock'** Pranjali woke up to the sound of someone at the door. Rubbing her eyes, she said, "Come in."

It was Vishwas, and she was surprised to see him at the hospital. She had assumed the villagers of Sampanpur might be celebrating their victory.

"Baba was worried about you," Vishwas said, stammering as he gathered the courage to speak. "After the argument that took place between you and Baba, he didn't have the courage to come here. He cares for his old friend."

"Tell him I shall never give up. I will get this investigated, and if no one supports me, I will do it alone. You can make a fool of the workers, but not me," she asserted.

"Absolutely not!" Vishwas responded, understanding Pranjali's anger. He was there to help her see that Sampat and the rest of Sampanpur cared for her. All they wanted was for Pranjali to stand by their side during this difficult time.

"Yes, that is true. Your father doesn't understand that I am struggling for your betterment; I have no selfish motive behind it. Do you not see that Sampanpur is still living a primitive life? You have no infrastructure, no facilities. You are left with nothing more than silly old folktales that have been passed down through generations. I can see that one more generation is on the verge of being wasted,"

Pranjali was panting by now. Vishwas moved to fetch her a glass of water. After taking a sip, Pranjali sighed.

"I understand that you care and think about our benefit. That is the very reason I am here. There are a few things you should know about Sampanpur."

"I am aware of all your fabricated stories. Let me make it clear: I do not believe them," Pranjali retorted. She lowered her tone and continued, "You should be happy that the government is eager to open new opportunities. Just think wisely—the beauty of Devshaila and Sampanpur will attract countless tourists. I understand you all love nature, so stick to it and embrace eco-tourism. Create resorts and home stays. Set your own rules. Earn some money and respect for yourselves."

Like his father, Vishwas never cared much for money.

"Well, our land has nurtured us for centuries, and we shall never destroy it for the sake of money. Masterji would have been very saddened if he were alive. He always supported and protected the tribals of Devshaila, and for that reason, every villager of Sampanpur stood by him. You should have taken the time to learn about him and his work. You know nothing about him. Before I leave, I want to share something very important with you: Devshaila is home to those tribals that your father supported and helped. Also, remember that those cries you hear are real. They can be heard whenever there is a danger to Devshaila."

With folded hands, he wished her goodbye and began to leave. As he reached the door, something held him back. He turned, looked into her eyes, and firmly said, "Not all places are meant for tourism. Some places must be preserved and reserved for future generations. We are working for that."

Vishwas left the hospital but left a bunch of questions for Mrunal, who was overhearing the conversation standing outside. She wondered what Vishwas meant by "the cries are real" and why her grandfather supported the mountain people.

Pranjali stayed in the hospital for two more days. Rishi had made up his mind that he wouldn't let Pranjali and Mrunal stay anywhere close to Mount Devshaila. He was firm to take them back home. But, Pranjali was reluctant. She wanted to stay back and so was Mrunal. Rishi knew that he could never be successful in convincing Pranjali to return. Also, Mrunal was as stubborn as her mother. Losing all weapons, he decided to stay back with them.

The accident brought a panic wave among all the labourers who were appointed for construction work at Devshaila. Anirudha and the Panchayat secretary were also disturbed. Pranjali reported the details to the Chief who found it difficult to believe. He thought that tumbling rocks might have hallucinated the laborers on that unfortunate day. The only relief was that no casualties were reported.

Mrunal wanted to meet Vishwas as soon as possible. She was eager to get some answers.

On the other hand, Pranjali wished to investigate the accident. She wondered if what she had witnessed was merely a hallucination or something more. Vishwas's words, "The cries are real," kept ringing in her mind. His mention of her father and his work left her with even more questions. Both mother and daughter had similar concerns; they knew that the answers they sought were buried somewhere on Devshaila, but setting foot there was impossible. They were left with only one option... Sampanpur.

Mrunal attempted to reach Vishwas, but he was avoiding her phone calls and texts, which made her restless and upset. After all, she couldn't be blamed for her mother's actions. Eventually, she decided to confront him in person. She arrived at the café in Devapur where she usually met him. As expected, Vishwas ignored her, so did their mutual friends who were present there. But Mrunal was not ready to give up so easily. She approached him directly and said, "What's wrong with you?" Stunned and embarrassed, he hurried to leave. Mrunal pursued him, yelling, "I'm talking to you!"

"Will you stop creating a scene? This isn't a big city like yours. Here, people notice even the smallest actions," Vishwas replied, exasperated.

Realizing how immaturely she behaved, she nervously muttered, "I'm sorry. I didn't mean to...You were avoiding me and...I was desperate to talk to you."

"Your mother..." saying this he turned his face away. "Did she send you?" he snapped.

"Why would she? I have nothing to do with her work. I wanted to meet you because I need certain answers."

Before Vishwas could respond, she quickly asked, "I overheard your and Mom's conversation the other day. All I want to know is: what more do you know about my grandfather? Also, what is the mystery behind the crying mountain?" She eagerly awaited Vishwas's answer while he struggled to process her rapid questions. After a long pause, he replied, "Have you ever visited your grandfather's house in Sampanpur? I suggest you do so."

"That's not the answer I was expecting."

"That's all I can say. Why don't you ask your mother or grandmother? Didn't they ever tell you that your grandfather worked for the welfare of the tribals of Mount Devshaila? He protected Devshaila and, in fact, gave up his life for that reason." His tone grew intense. Thinking he had already said too much, he turned and started walking away, but Mrunal followed him.

"Please stop following me. I don't trust you or your mother. Just go away. One more thing: ask her not to step on Devshaila. The tribals are enraged, and they won't spare her," he yelled.

Mrunal's eyes filled with tears. No one had ever spoken to her so harshly.

Rishi heard Mrunal weeping. He sneaked into her room as the door was ajar. Seeing him, she hugged him tightly and told him everything. She also said that she wished to visit her grandfather's house at Sampanpur. Rishi was taken aback to hear this. He couldn't stop himself from imagining Pranjali's reaction if Mrunal mentioned this to her. Pranjali storming around while Mrunal kept arguing with her was a picture that got painted in front of his eyes.

"Terrific!" he exclaimed.

"What?" Mrunal couldn't get his reaction.

Coming out of a dreadful imagination and without losing a second, he made it very clear to Mrunal that she must scrap Sampanpur out of her mind. He asked her not to mention Sampanpur to Pranjali. On hearing this, she was heartfelt but not lost. Troubled and fidgeting, she spent a sleepless night. First thing she wanted to do was to grab as much information as possible about her grandfather. She was always told that his death was an accident. Asking questions to her grandmother would raise an alarm, Mrunal thought. Best option was to visit her ancestral house in Sampanpur and for this, she needed someone trustworthy to accompany her. Rishi already knew about her intentions so he was the right person. Convincing him, was not very difficult.

Eventually after a lot of emotional drama and 'ifs-buts' Rishi agreed. He thought it would be safer for her to go with her father than meandering around in an unknown place.

The duo decided to keep their plans a secret from Pranjali and her mother. Rishi attempted to learn more about his father-in-law's work and ultimately chose to speak directly with his mother-in-law. Following the recent accident at the foot of Mount Devshaila, she felt it was necessary for the family to know about her late husband. It had been years since she had discussed Masterji with anyone. She was always proud of the respect he had earned, but she wanted to protect Pranjali from his research. She feared that Pranjali might become influenced by him, continue his research, and end up spending her life like Masterji did. As she spoke about him, her face reflected the pain of her grieving heart, revealing her deep sorrow for her late husband.

During their conversation, he discovered that Devshaila was no ordinary mountain; it was home to a variety of herbs and medicinal plants. A Sage who once lived on the mountain had taught the local tribes how to utilize those sacred plants, and this knowledge had been passed down through generations. Everything was fine until one unfortunate day, when a medicine was given to a child, resulting in the child losing all his senses. He acted as if he were possessed by a ghost.

Pranjali's father was a botanist who had a deep friendship with the local tribal people. He discovered that a child had been given medicine made from a contaminated herb. The pollutants emitted from the construction site in Devapur had harmed the delicate ecosystem of Devshaila. As a result, the tribals declared that area of the mountain to be impure, which is why they consistently opposed any construction activities nearby. Eventually, the entire community of Samapanpur vowed to protect Devshaila. While the world was evolving and adapting to new ways, Samapanpur chose to remain rooted in tradition. Pranjali's mother longed for a better life, but her husband was committed to their way of life in Samapanpur.

Pranjali's father cared deeply for the mountain people and conducted research with their help, though he never disclosed the specifics of his work. He would often say, "It is our duty to help them. They are working for a noble cause." He spent hours in his study, a room that was off-limits to others.

Rishi was honest enough to share this information with Mrunal, who quickly realized what Vishwas was implying. It became clear that Samapanpur was dedicated to protecting the ecosystem of Devshaila. Considering the fact, she thought that government should come up with such a solution that upbring Sampanpur and also preserve Mount Devshaila's ecosystem.

The information which she received about her grandfather made her curious to know about his research and that made her very much eager to visit her ancestral house.

On the other hand, Pranjali had an urgent meeting with the Chief for which she was required to travel to the city. Mrunal thought that this was the right opportunity to reach Sampanpur.

On the day Pranjali left for the meeting, Rishi and Mrunal decided to take action. Rishi knew that Pranjali would be upset if she found out about their visit to Sampanpur. However, he didn't want to let Mrunal go to an unfamiliar place alone, putting him in a difficult situation.

It was afternoon when they reached Sampanpur. Mrunal saw Vishwas coming towards them. Mrunal was happy and at the same time nervous to see him.

"Hi Vishwas!" Rishi greeted.

"Hello uncle, hope I'm not late" Vishwas smiled and replied.

Mrunal looked perplexed. "He's the right person to help us." Rishi whispered.

Soon, they were following Vishwas through the rough and uneven village terrain. The sun was shining brightly but the cold breeze added freshness in the air. Everything looked serene and pleasant. Mud houses surrounded with coconut and jackfruit trees stood proudly embracing the wind.

"Why is he helping us? And how did you convince him?" Mrunal curiously muttered.

"Well...I told him that you were willing to know your ancestry and so you wanted to visit the house" Rishi replied casually.

They reached the house after a short hike.

Vishwas asked Rishi and Mrunal to stay outside till he returns.

Vishwas went inside, there were children who were packing their books. A woman in her early 20's was about to lock the house. Vishwas asked her to hand over the keys to him. When she left, Vishwas signaled Rishi and Mrunal to get in.

"It's a school" Mrunal said surprisingly.

"It was your grandma's wish to turn it into a school. You can keep these keys; this house belongs to you" Vishwas said to Mrunal, handing out the keys. "Your paternal grandmother's wish", Vishwas made it clear to avoid any confusion.

"No, please keep it. We wished to visit it once. We are happy that it has served the best purpose ever" Rishi said.

Vishwas looked at Mrunal and tried to read her face. All this time, he has been trying to avoid looking at Mrunal but now he wanted to know what was on her mind.

Without a word, she stepped in. She touched the walls and windows as if she had been there before. She felt connected.

Whatever 2-3 rooms it had, were turned into classrooms except for one room. It was locked.

"Why is this room locked?" Mrunal asked

"This was once Masterji's research room. He would spend hours in this room. You shall find all his belongings inside. We kept it saved for his family to take over but none ever turned up" he replied sadly.

"Can you open it?"

Vishwas pulled out an old key from his pocket and opened it.

The room was dusty and dark. Rishi sneezed. The dust had turned his nose red.

"Dad, please wait outside" Mrunal insisted.

Rishi wasn't willing to leave Mrunal alone inside. He took out his handkerchief and covered his nose.

The room was filled with a variety of old items, all neatly arranged. However, the layer of dust clearly indicated that it had not been visited in years. Rishi opened the windows to let fresh air and light into the space. In one corner of the room stood a cupboard packed with files and old papers. Mrunal and Rishi began flipping through the pages and discovered several handwritten notes along with a collection of photographs. Some of the notes contained descriptions of various herbs, which Mrunal found particularly fascinating. She also noticed some symbols within the notes that were difficult to decipher. They spent a considerable amount of time exploring the items in the room. While Rishi explored the rest of the house, Mrunal remained busy in Masterji's room.

"Mrunal, soon it will be dark. We must return to Devapur" Rishi said, looking outside through the window.

"Oh... yes Dad. Can we carry this along?" she asked.

Her words alerted Vishwas.

"I request you not to carry anything outside. We have preserved this material for years. It may not be valuable to your mother but for us, it's a treasure. If you ever wish to see it again, you are welcome but nothing goes outside. Moreover, we don't trust your mother anymore." Vishwas stated before Rishi could say anything.

Rishi didn't counter Vishwas as he knew whatever Vishwas said was right. It was because of Sampat and his family that the house and Masterji's work was intact after all these years. They valued it.

"Well then, I found a reason to come back" Mrunal murmured, keeping all the stuff carefully inside the cupboard as she thought that Vishwas had a watch on her actions. Indeed, Vishwas was vigilant, he doubted that Mrunal might smuggled some stuff outside.

The files, documents and the photographs revealed a lot of things. Rishi and Mrunal were convinced by now that as believed by many people, Devshaila wasn't an ordinary mountain.

They thanked Vishwas for his help and left.

That night, before going to bed Mrunal asked Rishi if they could visit the house the next day as well. To her surprise, Rishi agreed readily. Pranjali was to return after two days so they had enough time, thought Rishi.

Mrunal spent the entire night browsing on the internet. Because, while she was going through her grandfather's documents something caught her eyes and that made her desperate.

The next morning, the duo left the house early.

"Dad, I think we should thoroughly check all the documents. If required we should also talk to someone who knows Sampanpur very well" Mrunal solemnly said.

"Are you and Vishwas still not on talking terms?" Rishi jested thinking that Mrunal was pointing towards Vishwas.

Mrunal was in no good mood. "Dad, I didn't contact him after that day. I intend to talk to someone who's senior in the village and knows grandpa very well" she looked irritated as she spoke.

"Sampat! Vishwa's father might help" Rishi said thoughtfully.

"I doubt. Especially after the aggressive step that mom took, I don't think he might even consider. I was astonished to see Vishwas yesterday. In fact, it's difficult for me to imagine the way you might have convinced him to come along with us."

"Well! That wasn't too difficult. And, don't worry. I'll take care of Sampat but before that, I'll have to contact Vishwas. We need the key to that room."

Vishwas was not at Sampanpur because he had some work to attend to, but he managed to arrange the keys for them as Rishi promised him that he or Mrunal would not carry away Masterji's work. Furthermore, Vishwas had no authority over Masterji's house so he didn't resist.

Mrunal and Rishi were once again inside Masterji's room. It looked just like they had the day before. Since it was Sunday, the school was closed, and there were no disturbances. Mrunal was searching for the document that had caused her to spend a sleepless night, but it was nowhere to be found. She felt anxious and continued to look in every nook and cranny of the room.

"Relax dear, it might be somewhere here. I hope you kept it safely yesterday"

"Yes Dad, I did but I couldn't find it" she replied anxiously.

Rishi asked her to describe the document to him.

"Dad, it had a picture of a fish with a scribble around it...Manu, Matsya, pralaya something of that sort was handwritten on it" the picture was very clear in front of her eyes.

Rishi was puzzled thinking what has it to do with the research of herbs. They opened each file but couldn't find anything. Rishi remembered coming across a photograph of an ancient script yesterday. He was sure someone must have purposefully taken it away. They both understood that Mrunal's grandfather wasn't just studying herbs but something beyond it.

Mrunal was resolute to uncover the truth.

Rishi and Mrunal reached Sampat's house, it was not too difficult for them to locate his place. Sampat and his family welcomed them. As expected, Vishwas wasn't at home.

Mrunal took a glance around, there was a huge painting of Bhagwan Vishu's Matsya Avatar which caught her attention.

"Did you like the painting?" Sampat asked

"Yes, it's beautiful. In fact, it was last night that I was reading on the internet about Matsya Avatar. Co-incidence, isn't it?" she fielded.

"Indeed! it is. Well! I'm happy that you visited your ancestral house." Sampat tried to change the subject.

Rishi was sitting by the window; he saw Vishwas outside. Now, it was time to touch the subject.

Rishi went close to the painting and observed it carefully. When Vishwas entered the house, he was stunned to see them at home. Moreover, seeing Rishi staring at the painting made him more restless.

Trying to act normal, he greeted Rishi and Mrunal. He went straight into the kitchen and gulped a glass of water.

"I am very grateful to Vishwas that he helped us. Mrunal was delighted to know that her grandfather was such a good botanist. We speak very little about him at home yet I believe, now she can connect with him" carefully touching the frame of the painting, he added, "I guess, she will love to study botany, Am I right, Mrunal?"

"Indeed, I'm willing to study. I was going through grandpa's research documents and I'm willing to study it deeply. In fact, we are here to know if he left any other documents in your possession. If it's with you please can you share those with us" Mrunal said looking at Sampat with great expectations.

"I'm glad to hear. All his belongings are kept in his room in your house... You shall find everything there itself" he replied.

"If you don't mind, can I please click a picture of this painting?" Rishi asked.

Mrunal was quick to observe the Vishwas's face turning pale.

Sampat simply nodded in agreement as Rishi pulled out his phone to take a snap.

Rishi and Mrunal had planned to stay at Sampanpur for the night. The next evening, Pranjali was about to return so whatever time was left, they wanted to utilize it properly. Sampat insisted that they stay at his place but Mrunal preferred staying at her grandfather's house.

After Rishi and Mrunal left, Vishwas heaved a sigh of relief. Sampat observed that it was unusual of Vishwas.

"What's wrong with you? Your face looks like a withered leaf"

"Baba, I made a blunder. I let them through Masterji's room without any thought" he took out some papers from his bag and handed them to Sampat. "I think Mrunal has seen this yesterday" Vishwas was sweating from head to toe.

Sampat was stunned to know this. This shouldn't have happened, he thought. No doubt, Rishi and Mrunal were staring at the painting. They were suspicious.

"Hide these papers. None should find them" he yelled.

"I'm sorry Baba" said Vishwas, looking abashed.

Vishwas was filled with guilt of being careless. He feared that the secret that was preserved for generations may get uncovered by his one silly mistake.

The next morning, Sampat and Vishwas visited Masterji's house. It was striking to see Masterji's room tidied up. Mrunal and Rishi had cleaned and arranged the room neatly.

They had studied all the documents the entire night but there was no trace of the missing document and photographs.

Mrunal handed over the keys to Vishwas, "My grandfather was brilliant and I'm proud of him. I shall pursue botany and continue with the research work that he left behind. I don't know...why was I always kept away from this place but I have decided to return to this house...Dad will support me. He promised."

Mrunal looked straight into Vishwas's eyes as she tried to clear her doubts, "Is there anything else that we are supposed to know?"

Vishwas couldn't answer this question looking into her eyes. There was certainly something important to tell but he couldn't. He was unable to trust her.

"All your answers lay in this room" he answered, taking a long breath.

Sampat could see his son getting nervous so to change the topic, he said, "Please give my message to your mother that some places don't like to invite people. Devshaila and Sampanpur can't be turned into tourist places. Moreover, we all are aware of how irresponsible some tourists are so we can't take any kind of risk."

Rishi knew Sampat had a point. Many places in the country faced the backslash of over tourism.

"Please make Pranjali understand this" he added further.

Rishi nodded as he had nothing to say further.

Rishi and Mrunal picked up their bags and reached the gates. Mrunal turned to the house with welled up eyes. She felt as if the house was asking her to stay behind. Rishi understood that his little daughter had found her calling.

Suddenly, he was stuck with a thought. He turned to Sampat, "I kept thinking of the painting that I saw at your house yesterday. I had heard stories of 'Dashavatar' as a child but with the course of time those stories just faded. Mrunal read a lot about it recently especially Matsya Avatar and she shared all the details with me. Also, let me tell you I am deeply fascinated with the story of the great Sage Manu."

Sampat was prepared for this. "Those are not mere stories. Matsya Avatar had a lot of responsibilities. Every time the earth takes *Jal Samadhi*, Bhagwan Vishnu in the form of a huge Matsya returns."

"Matsya!" exclaimed Rishi with a smile.

As Sampat and Vishwas walked back home, Sampat could read his son's distressed face. Placing his hand over Vishwas's shoulder he said, "Don't stress out. We all make mistakes. It's all because of you that the house which craved for its people had someone to visit it after decades. Besides, I could clearly read the girl's eyes and confirm that she is deeply touched. Also, she is attached to this place forever. I believe she will return. Unlike her mother, she seems to be more compassionate."

"But...Rishi Kaka has a hint I suppose" said Vishwas timidly.

"Hint of what? Nobody can ever imagine what dwells there. Let them make guesses and bring up theories. Nevertheless, we are prepared for everything, thanks to Masterji." Sampat winked and added, "Not all of his work is kept in his room, some I hid years back."

These words from his father sublimated Vishwas's stress. At last, there appeared a smile on his face and calmness in his mind.

"I shall send Raka the message that everything is fine here. Pranjali's daughter and husband have left. He will be relieved to know this" Sampat said.

Raka was the tribal chief of Mount Devshaila that guarded something very precious.

Mrunal and Rishi reached home. Pranjali arrived in the late evening. At the meeting, Chief asked Pranjali to hold on any kind of negotiations and talks with the villagers. It was time to take action, they concluded.

The labourers were terrified after the accident so it was necessary to first clear the fear that has spread in the air, the only way was by proving that there are no paranormal activities taking place on the mountain. According to the police report, it was a landslide that created havoc.

After a long time, Chief had come cross an officer who didn't believe in the stories of Devshaila and wanted to make use of it. It was decided that a team from head office would head to Devapur and blast a part of the mountain only to prove that the mountain is an ordinary one. Chief had faith in Pranjali and all the responsibility was given to her.

At the dinner when Rishi asked Pranjali about the meeting, she happily told him about the plan. Mrunal was at the table. She got restless on learning about the plan.

"Mom, when mountains are cut it destroys flora and fauna that housed them on its slopes for years. I mean... will it not damage the ecosystem?" she said looking apprehensively at Rishi.

"The thirst of development can only be quenched by sacrifice" Pranjali snapped. Realizing that it was rude of her to put such a statement, she added, "We shall take care of everything. Special care will be taken care of each living and non-living thing. For that, we need to investigate and research. If we don't step on that mountain then how can we understand the nature of the mountain? Moreover, it is also necessary to wash out the fear that resides in the people's heart."

Rishi couldn't accept her words.

"You couldn't step on it so you adopted the other way. To explode it?" he retorted

Mrunal was distraught to hear this.

"How could you do this mom?" she yelled.

"That's how things work dear. We have no other way. Those adamant villagers and tribals are just not willing to understand" Pranjali snarled.

In her heart, Mrunal knew Vishwas was right about her mother. She shall never understand the importance of Devshaila.

The next morning, Rishi overheard Pranjali talking to someone over phone that they would directly blast without stepping on it. The recent meeting with Chief made her more powerful, he thought. He asked Mrunal to contact Vishwas so that they could stay alert. He decided to be with Pranjali to keep an eye on her. He feared soon Pranjali might blast Mount Devshaila.

When Mrunal met Vishwas, she told him about her mother's thoughts. Vishwas wasn't surprised because he knew this was about to happen.

"For your mother's safety ask her to stay away. She isn't aware of the mountain people and their fury. They won't let anyone come close to the mountain. They stay hidden and their one arrow is enough to destroy your mother's intention," he warned.

"All I have to say is that I care of the mountain. I had studied grandpa's research. I understand the importance of the rare plant species that the mountain nurtures. I want to protect it at any cost. Dad and I stand by your side."

Vishwas was astonished to hear those words from her. It was paradoxical situation, mother trying to destroy while daughter was trying to protect. It was hard to believe.

"Please don't take Mom lightly. It seems that the department had given her more powers. If required, she may order direct blasts on the mountain without even stepping on it. I want you to be alert."

Vishwas understood the momentousness of her words. He reached Sampanpur at once. Mrunal accompanied him. They went to Sampat and informed him about Pranjali's plan. On hearing the dreadful news, Sampat was dumbstruck, "*Manu Matsya!*" were the words he spurted out of his mouth.

Mrunal couldn't understand anything. His words were jingling in her ears.

"Baba, don't worry. Nothing is going to happen to Manu Matsya."

"How can we fight? They are planning to blast it. That woman has no empathy" Sampat was broken. He couldn't believe that Masterji's daughter could ever do such a terrible thing.

"She won't be able to do anything. We shall fight together" Vishwas tried to calm him.

"You girl, I don't trust you" Sampat said pointing at Mrunal.

Mrunal trembled, her kind intentions were frequently questioned because of her mother.

"I am here to support and help you. Trust me. I know importance of Devshaila and its ecosystem. My grandpa did a great work and I want to take it forward. I can't let it get destroy" her tears gave witness of the purity of her intentions.

"Baba, she can help us. Even Rishi kaka is ready to support us. He is keeping a watch on Pranjali Ma'am" Vishwas said in Mrunal's support.

"In that case, it's time to tell her. She's Masterji's granddaughter. She needs to know" Sampat said standing in front of the Matsya Avatar's painting.

He asked Vishwas, to bring the documents and photographs that were hidden from Mrunal. He handed over those documents and photographs to Mrunal, "This belongs to Masterji, he was working for a bigger cause."

As she turned the pages and glanced through the photographs, her eyes widen.

To make things easier, Sampat said, "It's a deep hidden secret. These documents are about Manu Matsya. It dwells beneath the mountain. The sea that enters the mountain cave has been nurturing it and Devshaila has been protecting it for centuries. The great Sage who first arrived on Devshaila brought it along. He would address him by the name *'Manu Matsya'*. It is said that it was very tiny then. The Sage handed over the responsibility to protect the tiny creature to the tribal chief of Devshaila. He was told that it would leave this place when the right time comes. He readily accepted the responsibility and promised to fulfill it. It is till day that they are keeping their promise. We the villagers of Sampanpur have been friends with the tribals for years. Like them, we are deeply devoted to our 'Guru', our Sage. In fact, it was he who brought the two communities together. After he left us, we have been conjointly working to fulfill the responsibility that he handed over to the tribal chief. Vishwas told me once you are keen to know: 'why does the mountain cry?', let me tell you the reason today. It is not the mountain that cries, it's 'Manu Matsya'. Whenever, it senses any danger coming, it gives a loud cry. This alerts us. The day when you and your mother reached Devapur, it cried. It cried again on the day when Pranjali and her team tried to step on Devshaila."

Mrunal was overwhelmed to know this. The documents in her hand indicated that what Sampat said was right. Her grandfather had mentioned about sensibility and intelligence of 'Manu Matsya'. Those handwritten notes also mentioned that he was amazed to know that a living creature can stay alive through centuries. He also wondered about the mark on its head which resembles Bhagwan Vishnu's Tilak.

"Today I have revealed everything to you with the hope that you can make Pranjali understand the reason behind our stubbornness"

"Why didn't you tell her this secret? Had she known this..." she faintly uttered.

"Pranjali? Impossible!" exclaimed Sampat.

"Had she known this, she would have come with a group of scientists to conduct research on Matsya. We know her well." Vishwas responded.

Just then Mrunal's phone rang. It was her father.

"Hello Mrunal, where are you?" he asked.

"I'm at Sampanpur" she replied.

"That's nice. Listen to me carefully. Pranjali and her team are planning to blast the mountain tomorrow, this time with a better technology. It seems that her boss wants to start the road construction at the earliest. You try to collect the evidences of those rare plant species along with your grandpa's research work. I shall try to contact Ministry of Environment. I don't know how quickly will they respond but I should try. Meanwhile you please alert Vishwas and Sampat."

Mrunal was aghast to know this, she never expected her mother would be so quick in action.

"Ok Dad... I shall... do so..."

Rishi could sense the nervousness and fear in her voice.

"Mrunal dear, stay strong. I shall try to speak to Pranjali once again. Let's see if she changes her mind"

"Dad...dad...please wait until I return. We shall talk to her together" Mrunal spoke as she was stuck with an idea.

Vishwas and Sampat could read Mrunal's face. When Mrunal told them what Rishi said, they were shaken.

"The tribals shall wage war. They shall die but never let any harm come to Matsya. I must inform Raka at earliest. We need to be prepared" Sampat said breathing heavily. Looking at Vishwas he said, "Call for a meeting, we must first talk to all villagers"

When Vishwas was about to leave to inform everyone, Mrunal stopped him.

"I have a plan. Please handover grandpa's research work to me" taking a pause, she added "I have a way to convince her." Handling back the documents and photographs of 'Manu Matsya' to Vishwas she said, "You never told me about Matsya. I'm only struggling to save the mountain because it has a treasure of rare plants species and any human intervention can harm them. As mentioned, in these research papers any kind of pollution around this region can harm the plants thus changing the chemical composition in them and making them toxic. Conclusively, tourism should never take roots in this zone and if it does, we shall lose the ecosystem here. I shall share this theory with Mom. Meanwhile, dad shall use his contacts in ministry to stop the blast"

Mrunal's words brought a hope and smile to Sampat's face.

"Does that mean you'll be keeping the secret of Matsya from your mother?" Vishwas asked surprisingly.

"Some secret needs to be preserve. Perhaps that was the reason that my grandpa didn't even talk about it to my grandma."

Vishwas gave her Masterji's research work excluding the information about 'Manu Matsya'.

"You be alert. I shall soon contact you" saying this she hastened.

"One important thing, please see that this issue doesn't spread on social media. If this goes viral, so-called nature loving enthusiasts shall gather around and make things worse. We can't take risk of scientists and researchers coming here. This place must remain isolated. To protect Matsya, we must keep scientists or environmentalist away." Vishwas mentioned quickly as she was about to leave.

Vishwas was right. If the information that Devshaila holds rare medicinal plants leaks outside, many pharma companies would pounce upon it. Mrunal had to think quickly over it. She called her dad and without talking much she asked him to not to inform anybody at ministry about Devshaila.

Soon she reached home but chose not to mention anything about Matsya to Rishi.

"Why did you stop me from making a contact at the ministry?" mystified, he questioned on seeing Mrunal.

She took a deep breath, hiding things from her father was difficult for her but it was the only way to maintain secrecy of Matsya.

"If the truth about medicinal plants leaks out then the researchers would flock around Devshaila. If not tourism then pharma industries would ultimately destroy it for their benefit" she answered.

"Don't be silly Mrunal. If the plants are so valuable then the entire human race must get benefit from them"

"But, those tribals have been living there for centuries. Devshaila is their home. We can't break into their houses for our greed. There are many places which are turned into crematorium because of greed and I don't want Devshaila to turn into it. They are innocent people, living peacefully. They aren't asking us for anything. They are just safeguarding and keeping their share of natural resource. Can't we just stop snatching what's not ours? Let's not spoil another green patch."

"These are very nice lines and fits well for school essay. Just grow up. Those rare plants can save million lives. They can help us treat many neurological disorders"

"And if those gets into wrong hands, will it not give rise to a new bioweapon?"

Rishi was startled on hearing these words. 'Bioweapon', Mrunal was right. The chemicals from those plants could be used to create a bioweapon. How difficult it was for any scientist to play with human mind and emotions using those chemicals? Masterji's research work also mentioned about it.

His eyes widened and the sweat made its way from his forehead to his cheek. Her words unnerved him.

"Dad...Dad"

"I never thought of this. It could be a disaster" he mumbled.

Taking her father's hand in her hand, Mrunal, said "Dad, perhaps grandfather knew this so he hid his research."

They had very less time as the blast was to take place tomorrow, without any talks or negotiations with the tribals. They both thought but found it difficult to approach Pranjali. Rishi feared if she comes to know about the plants, she would inform Chief. This would give him a valid reason to carry on all the research activities.

It was dinner time; everyone was at the dinner table but Mrunal didn't turn up. To check on her, Pranjali went to Mrunal's room and found her crying.

With concern, she asked her the reason. Mrunal hugged her tightly and cried more.

"What's the matter child?" she asked apprehensively.

"Mom, please don't blast the mountain" Mrunal sobbed.

"Oh! Don't worry dear, this time we have come up with a new technology. Nothing shall harm your mother. Everything shall go smoothly" she tried to pacify Mrunal thinking that she was worried for her especially after the accident.

Just then Rishi entered the room.

"You can't blast the mountain" he declared.

He handed over Masterji's research work to her.

"No dad!" Mrunal panicked.

"Mrunal, we shouldn't hide. In fact, we must help her to broaden her vision and think beyond the materialistic gains. And, for that she needs to check on these documents. Perhaps then, let her decide if she wants to destroy that mountain or protect it." Rishi said looking into Pranjali's eyes.

Taking the documents from Rishi, Pranjali began turning the pages and was surprised by what she found. She carefully investigated the contents, which seemed lucid and clear to her. More importantly, she understood the core reason behind the resistance of the tribals and villagers of Sampanpur to any activities around the mountain. Regret filled her as she realized that she had always focused on the superficial aspects instead of delving deeper into the issue. She had never attempted to uncover the reasons behind the protests.

"How did you get this?" she asked in a shaky voice.

Rishi explained that Mrunal had overheard the conversation between Vishwas and her at the hospital. She was determined to visit her grandfather's house to learn more about him. Eventually, they went to Sampanpur, where Rishi informed her that the villagers had transformed the house into a small school and had preserved Masterji's belongings in his room. Pranjali was shocked when Rishi mentioned that Vishwas had the key to that room and had helped them gain access. As Rishi recounted how events unfolded, a sense of respect grew within Pranjali for Sampat.

Rishi made her understand that if the research papers were leaked, the entire mankind shall have to face its adverse consequences.

The fact that she never tried to know about her father and his work, filled her heart with remorse. She regretted for not even visiting their house at Sampanpur when she had a chance to do so. She remembered that the way she ignored it when Sampat asked her to pay a visit the last time, she was at Sampanpur.

It was a tough night for Pranjali. How was she going to stop the blast?? She had immediate orders from the Chief to undertake the task at the earliest. She cursed herself for this. After the accident, the Chief was very much convinced to step back after the labourers mentioned of witnessing the Sage's spirit on the mountain but Pranjali protested that it was a mere hallucination. Situation wouldn't be complex had she known about the reality of Mount Devshaila earlier, she thought to herself.

The only option left with her was to use the most dreadful weapon which kept Devshaila safe all these years- 'Fear'.

Later, she went into her room to get some sleep. Rishi was already asleep.

It was 3:00 AM when Mrunal woke up hearing someone scream. It was Pranjali, she was petrified and was howling in fear. Rishi found it very difficult to handle her. Pointing towards the window, she yelled, "He has come to take me. He knows about the blast."

Pranjali's mother understood what she was pointing at.

"No one is taking you away from us" she broke into tears.

All this commotion woke up the neighbours. Soon everyone was able to hear the cries from the mountain. This created a scary atmosphere.

By the morning, the news spread like a forest fire. All credit to the housemaid who didn't take much time to spread the news that Pranjali had seen the Sage's spirit and he is after her life. This created panic among the neighbours. The officers and the labourers who were supposed to join Pranjali and her team for the blast were horrified to learn this. Besides, they had already heard the horrendous cries from the mountain last night.

The doctor was called upon to check Pranjali. He injected her with some medicine so that she could rest. Anirudha was now the in-charge of the operation but he had no courage to set a foot near Devshaila. He at once rushed to dial Chief's number and briefed him everything. The Chief who had already heard many stories was taken aback. Considering Pranjali's confidence at the last meeting, he had a lot of expectations from her. She was his last hope. Eventually, he was left with no option but to call off the operation. Anirudha was relieved to hear it. Chief instructed him that Pranjali be given the best medical treatment and for that he asked to arrange her travel back to the city. Pranjali who was still under the shock was unable to assimilate anything. Rishi was worried for her. He knew Pranjali was under a lot of stress and that has taken away her peace. By the afternoon, their bags were packed and they were all set to leave. Mrunal was troubled, she blamed herself for her mother's condition. Soon their car arrived and all the luggage was dumped in. Before leaving Mrunal had a very important phone call to make. She called up Vishwas and shared both good and the bad news. Though Vishwas was relieved that all the construction activities at Devshaila were halted till indefinite time, he was concerned for Pranjali. Especially, after knowing that Mrunal had revealed about Masterji's research to her.

During their journey Pranjali didn't speak a word. Rishi was deeply hurt to see her condition. On reaching the city, she was immediately rushed to the hospital. The Chief had already fixed the appointment with the 'best neurologist' in the city. Everything at the hospital went smoothly. The doctor advised her rest and no stress at all. He specially mentioned to avoid talking about the accident in her presence as that would trigger her anxiety and may repeat the similar attack. Rishi and Mrunal made a note of it.

At home, Pranjali had a few visitors, mostly colleagues and friends. They were already requested to not talk about work or any related topic. Pranjali spent most of day sleeping in her room. It was the effect of the medications that she was taking.

One day, she saw Mrunal crying in her room.

"What's wrong my child?" she asked her.

Mrunal never wanted her mother to see her cry. She quickly wiped away her tears and made excuses. Pranjali on the other hand was aware of her daughter's pain.

"I know, you are worried for me. It has been fifteen days that you all are struggling to see me at peace" Pranjali said. "You need not worry and stress out. I'm absolutely fine" she added as she sat on an armchair.

Mrunal smiled gently. She rested her head on her mother's lap. It has been a while that Mrunal felt so comfortable and warm. No matter how big the problems are but a gentle touch from mother always brings calmness and warmth.

"When was the last time you spoke to Vishwas? I hope everything is fine at Sampanpur", Pranjali asked.

Mrunal felt a sudden bolt of thunder stuck under her nerve. It was first time in fifteen days that Pranjali had enquired about anybody. Mrunal wanted to avoid the question. Before she could make an excuse, Pranjali said, "How is the situation there? I hope everything is stopped and the project file is dumped somewhere. You must find its status for me." Mrunal was dumbstruck. "Was she getting normal? Or was her condition deteriorating?" she said to herself.

Mrunal was perplexed. Pranjali could read her mind. "Mrunal, I'm perfectly fine. I played. I had no other option to stop the project. I believe, I was successful to sustain the fear that was already housed in the minds of the labourers and the officers. I guess, now the Chief also believes in the story of the Sage. If he isn't convinced, I will have to continue this way." Mrunal couldn't believe her ears.

"Mom, you were acting?"

"I did... I'm sorry, I hid it from you and Rishi. I was supposed to be realistic."

"Mom, you risked your health, your career. What if you were treated with extreme doses of medicines?"

"I had no other way. I am doing it for my baba. This is the least I could do. I know Chief very well. He could have gone to any extend had he come to know about baba's research."

Mrunal's eyes were flooded. She hugged her mother tightly. Her heart was filled with pride.

"As a child, I once heard my grandmother telling my mother that some stories need to remain alive for the protection of mankind. I believe she was pointing to the story of the Sage. I guess, my mother is also the one among many who kept those stories alive but she chose a different path."

Sampat was happy that all the machines were pulled away from the foothills of Devshaila. But, the tribals were watchful. They wanted no risk. Vishwas was relaxed but was concerned for Pranjali. He didn't receive any message or call from Mrunal after she left. Sampat asked him to contact Mrunal but he hesitated. Finally, Vishwas decided to have a word with Mrunal and dialed her but she didn't receive his call. This created a sense of fear in his mind. He silently prayed for Pranjali. Just then there was a beep on his phone. It was a message from Mrunal. It said, "Please take me in. I want to be part of Sampanpur. I shall work along with you people to protect Matsya."

"No, you can't. It will be difficult for you" he replied.

"Nothing can be more difficult than standing under the scorching sun with two huge luggage bags and waiting for you to take me in."

He rushed to the door and there she was standing in front of him to be part of the mission to protect 'Matysa' till the time to come.

TWO

THE BROKEN TOOTH

Two sisters, Meera and Mahi were playing outside their house. Suddenly, Mahi complained of having a toothache. Meera who was six years older than Mahi examined her mouth like a dentist and declared that she was about to lose her first milk tooth.

What should I do with that broken tooth?" Mahi asked innocently.

"If you bury your broken tooth in the soil, a pearl bearing plant shall grow out of it" Meera said. "But keep in mind that the tooth should not be pulled out forcefully" she warned Mahi.

Mahi was excited to hear this.

The girls had watched their mother toil day in and day out to make a living. She worked hard to raise them ever since their father left for the city, promising to return with a lot of money. However, he never fulfilled his promise and never came back home.

"What will you do with those pearls, Mahi dear?" Meera asked playfully.

"Oh! Let me think" after a while she replied, "I shall make a pearl necklace for Amma. She has no jewellery except for the yellow thread that she wears around her neck" Meera smiled to this.

Everyday Mahi would observe her loose tooth in the mirror before going to school. She waited for it to come out. At times, she would think of pulling it out but recalling Meera's warning she hesitated.

Mahi, being timid and a shy girl, was often bullied at school by a boy named Raka. He would beat her, pull her hair and snatch her lunch box away.

Meera was aware of her sister's sufferings. She made her understand that it is necessary to fight back such bullies using mental strength rather than physical strength.

One day at school while Mahi was having her lunch, Raka tried to snatch her lunch box. But Mahi decided not to give up this time. She had observed that Raka always kept a pen in his shirt's pocket. In fact, she had heard other children say that it was his lucky charm and he loved it above everything.

"This is his weakness," Mahi thought.

No sooner did Raka come closer to grab Mahi's lunch box, she stretched her little arm and pulled Raka's pen from his pocket. She was so swift that Raka was unable to figure out anything.

Raka was successful in snatching Mahi's lunch box but his lucky pen was seized. Helplessly, he saw Mahi fiddle the pen between her fingers. Unwillingly, he had to let go of Mahi's lunch box in exchange for his pen. Everyone witnessed Mahi's bravery and praised her for it. But the act left Mahi with a bleeding mouth. Her loose tooth fell out of its arrangement. Her friends gathered around her to check on her but Mahi was not interested. She was worried about losing her broken tooth; she kept looking for it on the floor. Desperately, she looked for it because without her first milk tooth, she would not be able to get a pearl bearing plant. All her efforts were futile. She lost her milk tooth and cried a lot over the loss.

Crying, she returned home from school and narrated the entire incident to Meera. Meera was proud of her sister who acted so bravely and faced the bully but was saddened to see Mahi's tears. She tried hard to comfort Mahi but failed.

In the evening when mother returned home, she cooked Mahi's favorite dish to make her happy but nothing brought a smile to her face. That night, Mahi slept with tears in eyes.

The next morning when Mahi woke up, a bright smile appeared on her face. She found a packet full of white shining pearls under her pillow.

She ran out screaming and jumping with joy.

"Meera Akka! Look I got the pearls, I found them under my pillow" Mahi joyfully said.

"Such lovely pearls! I guess it is a gift from the fairy. She might have seen you courageously face Raka, so without bothering for the broken milk tooth, she gifted you this bunch of pearls," said Meera as she planted a kiss on Mahi's forehead.

Mahi's happiness knew no limits. She threaded the pearls into a string and gifted those to her mother.

Mother was overwhelmed. Big drops of tears appeared in her eyes. She hugged her daughters as she knew one had threaded the pearls while the other one had broken her piggy bank for the sake of those pearls.

THREE

REBORN TO BE CALLED AS 'CHINNA KAVERI'

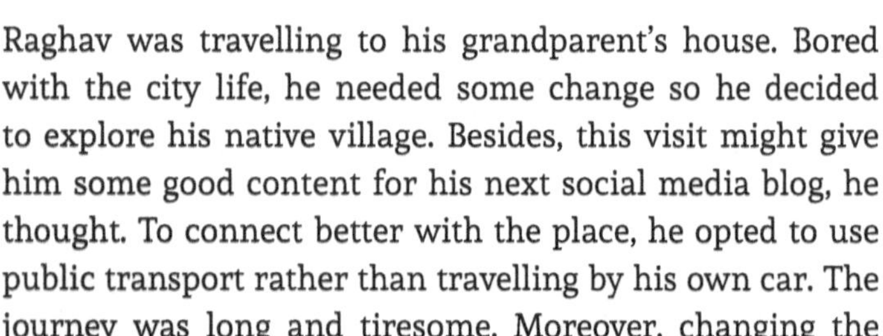

Raghav was travelling to his grandparent's house. Bored with the city life, he needed some change so he decided to explore his native village. Besides, this visit might give him some good content for his next social media blog, he thought. To connect better with the place, he opted to use public transport rather than travelling by his own car. The journey was long and tiresome. Moreover, changing the buses in-between made him even more exhausted.

After Raghav reached the village, he was warmly welcomed by his grandparents. Their happiness had no limits. The news of his arrival was known to every single living being in the village. To his surprise, as he walked through the dusty lanes, every passer-by greeted him with a bright smile. However, he was amazed to know that everyone knew him because last time when he visited them, he was just five.

Though he was always away from his grandparents, he loved them dearly. He wanted them to stay with him in the city but they weren't willing to embrace the city life.

Raghav's grandparents had a modest house with a nice and well-maintained front yard which had a full-grown mango tree apart from many other plants. The entrance of the house was decorated with a rangoli. In fact, it was his grandmother's practice to wake up and bath before the sunrise, followed by cleaning the front yard and putting rangoli to start the day.

Raghav enjoyed his stay as he was most pampered and loved. Grandma prepared delicious traditional dishes, while Grandpa shared captivating stories from Raghav's father's childhood.

He spent his days exploring various parts of the village, and the fresh, serene environment allowed him to forget the toxicity of city life. Among all the places he visited, the bank of the river attracted him the most. This spot was remarkably clean and beautiful, unlike many other areas in the country. The water was so clear that the riverbed was visible, and the reflection of the emerald green mountain on the opposite bank added to the scenery. Raghav was truly impressed by the beauty of this place, as he had never encountered anything like it before.

Each morning, he would visit the river. Sitting there alone, he found the space to introspect and reflect on his life. There was an enigmatic magic in the air that helped him understand the rhythm of his heart. In essence, the place provided him with a kind of "mantra" for self-understanding and self-analysis.

The night was about to fall and Raghav was nowhere to be seen. Worried, his grandma tried calling him but the network being poor, she couldn't reach him. After a considerable amount of time, grandpa decided to step out and look for him. As he was about to leave, Raghav appeared at the door. Both the grandparents gave a sigh of relief.

"Where were you all this time? We were so worried for you" said his grandma with concern.

"Oh! I was by the river" Raghav replied casually as he made his way into the house

"At this hour?"

"Yes" he answered, sipping a glass of water. He noticed that grandma's face grew pale.

"I do not want you to visit that place again." grandpa said gravely as he went into his room and closed the door with no further word.

Raghav found it to be weird and with a puzzled face he looked at his grandma for an answer. Though grandma's face had a lot to tell, she hesitated to exchange words with him. She served him dinner and went to her bed.

Raghav found his grandparent's behaviour to be mysterious.

Next morning, he overheard his grandpa saying, "We must see that he doesn't go to the river again. Young and curious minds often have tendency to invite danger"

"This is it. There is a mystery and a new story for my content" Raghav thought. He was eager to seize the opportunity. He was sure that talking to grandpa over the topic wouldn't be fruitful. So, he tried to approach his grandma for an answer.

After lunch when grandpa went into his room for his afternoon nap, Raghav took a chance. He looked for his grandma all over the house and finally found her sitting under the mango tree in the front yard.

He approached her with his question as to why he was asked to stay away from the river but she was reluctant to give him any satisfactory answer. Eventually, tired with her unacceptable replies, he declared, "If you don't tell me the reason, I won't stop going there"

Grandma had no option but to tell him the reason. She asked him to follow her outside the house. After a walk they reached the river bank. As expected, there was no one around except for the cool breeze that welcomed them. Pointing towards the mountain on the other side of the river she said, "Do you see that mountain?"

To this, Raghav nodded in agreement.

"There was a village named Kodaigramam at the foothills of that mountain which now lies sunken under the water."

On hearing this, Raghav's eyes grew wider.

"How did that happen?"

"This is 'Kal-yuga', my child. The 'Rakshashas' live among us, very close to us. There was one such 'Rakshash' who entered Kodaigramam to destroy it forever. The village which was once lively and cheerful, has no existence today because of him" saying that she turned silent.

"Tell me more" Raghav insisted.

She once again looked at the mountain and said, "Kodaigramam, was a gifted village. Its land was fertile enough to bring life to any seed that was sowed. The river gave the villagers water for their farms and the mountain gave them protection.

People there grew mangoes, the most delicious and juicy mangoes I have ever tasted. The mango tree that you see in our front yard belongs to the same mango family" a drop of tear rolled out of her eye.

"There used to be a 'setu'... a bridge...that connected our village with Kodaigramam. I was a little girl then. I would often visit the Kodaigramam with my Appa(father). Everything was merry and beautiful until he arrived, Virasen. He was the distant cousin of the village-head. He came to the village with an ambition to conduct research on the mangoes that grew in abundance on that fertile land. He had various plans to export mangoes and mango-based products to other countries. He was a witty fellow and it wasn't difficult for him to convince the villager for it. Creating an illusion that his plan would bring wealth and prosperity into each house, he won their respect and trust.

Virasen needed land to establish a factory for his research and processing work. Driven by greed, the villagers willingly handed over their land to him. Eventually, the factory was built on the fertile and rich land of Kodaigramam. Many outsiders visited the factory, including researchers and scientists. It provided employment to the village's working class, who would otherwise have worked on the landlord's fields for meager wages. Local residents secured jobs with a steady monthly salary that was unattainable through farm labor. Many were hired to excavate the land. Without questioning or understanding what was happening inside the factory, the workers continued to dig and follow orders.

The village had a temple on the bank of the river. Next to the river, the temple priest lived with his only daughter, Chinna. She was an innocent girl with a pure soul. She had a special liking for the river and would spend hours staring at it.

One day, she noticed some strange activity happening in the river. The river which was always clean and clear, had suddenly changed its colour.

The ones who drank the water from the river got seriously ill. Chinna was disturbed by this. She wanted to understand the reason for the river turning toxic. Later, she found that the waste from the factory was dumped into the river. She went to the village-head to inform him but he dispelled her saying that 'Spending all her day staring at the river had turned her insane.'

She went door-to-door trying to make people understand the harm that the factory was causing to the village and the river but none believed her. There were some who believed her but had no nerve to go against the village-head. With no support from the villagers, she alone headed to the factory. Thereafter, she never returned home. She just disappeared. Her poor father looked for her everywhere but couldn't find her.

The condition of Kodaigramam was getting worst day by day. People stopped getting remuneration for their work. They were treated like animals. Eventually, they were turned into slaves.

Virasen was digging the earth for something and sending it to various places. The village-head was making profit and stood by his side. Together, they suppressed the voices that were raised against them.

Days passed by but the factory didn't stop spitting venom. The river turned dark and filthy. The mango trees gradually started losing lives and so did the people of Kodaigramam. Cries could be heard from every house. Entire Kodaigramam was enveloped by a blanket of smoke, dust, hunger, pain and cries of the victims.

Silently, the river kept shallowing the filth and venom churned out of the factory until one day, it became unbearable. It took the form of goddess 'Kali' to slay the demons. The clouds thundered and light struck like never before. Huge waves rose in the river. People ran for their lives. The river had entered the village looking for the 'Rakshasas,' ready to wash them away.

Virasen, the researchers, scientist, the village-head and his followers tried to climb the mountain for safety. But the river opened its mouth wide and gulped them. The entire village was submerged under the water but the innocent ones survived to tell the story.

They say, when the water started rising Chinna appeared out of nowhere and helped the poor villagers to climb up the mountain. After the people reached a safe place, she vanished mysteriously.

After the turbulent river returned to its usual form, the rescue operation was given a jump start to bring the stranded people from the mountain to the safe location.

A team of officers was appointed by the government to investigate the tragedy but none was able to find the reason behind the sudden rise in water level of the river. The unique phenomenon of nature surprised everyone. Apart from this, an important thing was observed, most of the villagers were saved except for a few. The officers found it suspicious but couldn't reach a conclusion.

The rescued villagers of Kodaigramam spoke of Chinna helping them. Many who had assumed she was dead believed it was her spirit that aided them, while others thought she was alive and hiding somewhere in the mountains. They all felt a deep gratitude toward her, as well as guilt for not supporting her when she had pleaded for help. It seemed that the river had come to her aid, which perhaps explained why the culprits were punished by its waters. From that day forward, the villagers began calling the river 'Chinna Kaveri' in her honor.

Few days later, people noticed that only the name of the river hadn't changed but its nature had also changed. She never allowed any one to carry out any activity in the water. No boats allowed; no fishing allowed. And most importantly if anyone would try to make it filthy, 'Chinna Kaveri' would engulf that person. She permits us to only use the water but never to spoil it"

Raghav was overwhelmed. A content creator within him was deeply impressed by the story. He suspected it to be a cooked-up story by someone only to create terror among the villagers. Nevertheless, at least the fear that was created, has helped to keep the river and its surrounding clean, he thought.

"There might be records in the government office if you wish to check about the tragedy," grandma tried to make it clear.

Raghav didn't wish to hurt his grandma by opposing her on any point so he convincingly said, "I do not doubt the story. Trust me, I believe you. I also understand if it had not been for 'Chinna Kaveri' this beautiful place would have been turned into an unpleasant dumped yard long back."

"Thank you. I hope your questions are answered well. Let's return home. The sun is about to set."

As both turned their backs to return, a huge wave arose from the river. Raghav noticed some movement in the water so he turned again to check. Trembling like a withered leaf, he stood petrified looking at the wave. However, grandma continued walking towards home, "I guess, she has come to testify the story" after a pause while still walking, she said, "Chinna, he is my grandson."

Finally, Raghav had a new content but he wasn't willing to make a video and make it viral as he knew if he did, millions of followers might flock into the village and make it a hotspot for their social media posts. In a way, he wanted peace to remain and no tragedy to take place.

It was the time for Raghav to return. Saying good-bye to his grandparents and 'Chinna Kaveri,' he left with a bunch of memories.

A year later, there was a knock on the door. It was the postman with a registered post. Grandparents were happy to know that it was from Raghav. Eagerly, grandma opened it. To her surprise, it was a book with the title ***Reborn to be called as Chinna Kaveri'** by Raghav Chandran.*

FOUR

The Empty Plate and a Yellow Flower

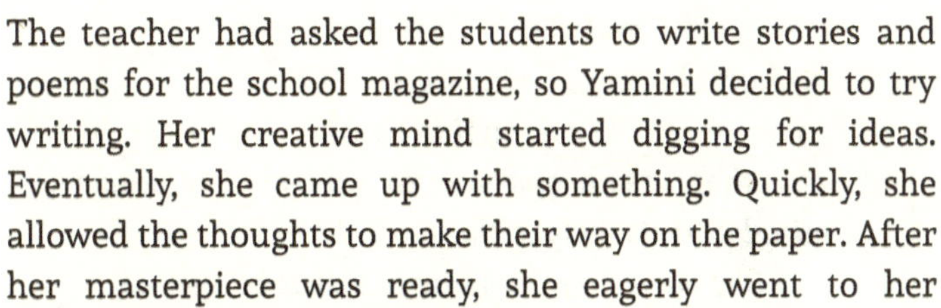

The teacher had asked the students to write stories and poems for the school magazine, so Yamini decided to try writing. Her creative mind started digging for ideas. Eventually, she came up with something. Quickly, she allowed the thoughts to make their way on the paper. After her masterpiece was ready, she eagerly went to her grandmother to share it with her.

"Granny! I have written something for the school magazine. Would you like to hear it?"

"Oh! I would love to hear it," said Grandmother enthusiastically.

Yamini smiled brightly and cleared her throat. "The title is '*The Empty Plate and a Yellow Flower*.'" She waited for a second and looked at her grandmother to check if she liked the title.

"That is interesting!" exclaimed the grandmother.

Back to her reading, Yamini continued,
*"All these years, she struggled to drive it off but it was
stubborn enough to stay along.*
*Its sheer sight brought havoc in the house with frightening
cries and screams around.*
Seasons changed and she was left alone in a sizable house.
*None to talk to and none to laugh with, she silently spent
her friendless moments.*
*For months, she had no visitors until one night, she saw the
same old tiny monster around.*
*Wandering for food, it swiftly ran into the kitchen, feasting
on whatever was available.*
She gently dropped a spoonful of leftover mashed potatoes.
And, observed her visitor standing at a distance.
Her withered lips smiled as her guest nibbled happily.
*'Squeak' 'Squeak' it thanked the kind lady for the delicious
meal she fed him.*
Gradually, it became a routine.
*Each night, she cooked potatoes and left them on a plate for
her teeny tiny guest.*
*House that was always deserted suddenly had people to
mingle but the lady of the house departed forever.*
She passed on the house to a distant cousin.
*But, before her final moments, she made a request, 'Every
night, please keep a spoonful of mashed potatoes at the kitchen
counter.'*
*Though it was strange, the new owner of the house
promised to practice.*
*As usual, at midnight, the mouse hopped into the kitchen,
had his share, and left without being noticed.*
*The next morning, everybody was stunned to see the empty
plate in the kitchen and a yellow flower next to the lady's
picture.*

*They made inquiries but nothing was brightened. Years passed by but this continues..., **'the empty plate and a yellow flower'** the mystery remains forever."*

Yamini's writing had made grandmother remember someone. She got immersed in her own thoughts. On noticing this, Yamini asked," What happened granny? Didn't you like it?"

"Dear! It is nothing like that. Your words made me remember Godavari Amma"

"Who is she?"

"Godavari Amma! Oh! She lived in our village. Let me tell you her story."

"When I was a young girl, an old woman named Godavari Amma lived in our village. She was a kind-hearted woman who would feed the hungry and help those in need. After her only son was martyred in a war, she was left all alone.

Godavari Amma was not a particularly religious person. She never attended religious ceremonies at the temple, and no one ever saw her praying. Despite this, every afternoon, she would carry a plate of the food she cooked to the village temple as an offering to '*Bhagwan Vishnu*'. To everyone's surprise, the plate was always empty by the evening. All the villagers believed that it was '*Bhagwan Vishnu*' who accepted Godavari Amma's offering, but she knew who had truly taken the food.

There was a young boy who worked at the cycle shop near the temple. He hardly spoke to anyone; however, he was hardworking and never gave anyone a reason to complain. Like Godavari Amma, he had no family. She knew the boy was the one who emptied her plate of offerings, but she pretended not to notice him. Once, she tried to make eye contact with him but he turned away. Despite this, she continued bringing him delicious food because she loved to feed him.

It once happened that Godavari Amma was unable to carry the plate to the temple for several days. The boy grew restless, but it wasn't just because he missed a free meal; he was genuinely concerned for her. He went to Godavari Amma's house and found the door closed. The window was open, and he saw her lying on the bed, crying in pain. He immediately rushed to fetch the doctor. The doctor examined her and gave her a painkiller that provided relief. He advised her to rest. The boy visited her every day to check on her but he never entered the house. He would only watch her from the window and leave after confirming her condition.

Godavari Amma gradually recovered. She soon noticed that someone was leaving fruits and milk at her doorstep every day.

Eventually, Godavari Amma resumed her routine of carrying the plate to the temple, but she could no longer see the boy at the cycle shop. Upon enquiring with the shop owner, she learned that he had returned to his village because his mother was unwell. Godavari Amma felt saddened that she had missed the opportunity to thank him, as he was the one who had called the doctor and saved her life. Even though she knew the boy was not in the village, she continued carrying the plate to the temple. To her surprise, she found it empty each evening. At first, she was astonished, but later she thought that her food might have satisfied the hunger of some needy.

One day, while walking around the village, Godavari Amma saw the doctor who had treated her a few days earlier. Thinking she should thank him for his kind help, she approached him and said, 'Thank you Doctor, it is all because of your timely treatment that I'm alive today'.

The doctor looked puzzled and replied that he had never visited her or treated her, as he had not been in the village that day. Godavari Amma was stunned to hear this. Although she had been extremely unwell that day, she was certain it was this doctor who treated her, and she remembered the boy standing by her bedside. Confused, she continued walking toward her house. On the way, she passed the cycle shop and overheard the owner say, 'Vishnu was very hardworking and innocent. It is hard to find help like him. I hope he returns.' "

Yamini was deeply touched on hearing her grandmother's story.

"Did Vishnu return to the village?" Yamini asked emotionally.

To this grandmother replied, "he didn't but the villagers say, Godavari Amma's offerings were always accepted at the temple."

FIVE

THE SEED THAT HELPED TO HEAL

Keshav and Madhav were twin brothers who disliked each other and often fought over trivial matters, which worried their mother. She noticed that other boys would take advantage of their rivalry, deceiving the brothers and instigating fights between them. Despite her numerous attempts to end the daily quarrels, her efforts proved fruitless. As the days passed, nothing changed between the brothers.

One day, their mother fell very ill. Unable to get out of bed, she called her sons to her side and asked them to go to the forest to fetch some firewood. Before they left, she made them promise, "Children, promise me that you will not go deep into the forest and that you will stay together."

Keshav and Madhav agreed.

They walked towards the forest. Both hesitated to walk together, as being together was nothing less than a punishment. Keshav walked ahead while Madhav sauntered after him.

"Stop dawdling! We don't have all day", Keshav hissed.

"I am walking at my own pace. Had it not been for my mother's promise, I would have never come along with you," Madhav said abruptly.

Arguing and quarrelling, they reached the forest.

A sage who was meditating under a tree was disturbed by their presence. Keshav and Madhav's arguments caught his ears. He watched them but refrained from preaching them.

The sun was about to set. Keshav and Madhav gathered as much firewood as they could and returned home.

Weeks later, the sage appeared at their doorsteps asking for alms. Since their mother was still unwell, Madhav offered the sage some rice. Looking at the rice, the sage said,

"Seems that your mother is still unwell."

Madhav was surprised to hear this. He wondered how the sage knew about Mother being unwell.

"Yes, she isn't doing well. But, how did you...?" Madhav hesitated and couldn't complete the question.

"How did I know about her is not important? What you can do for her is more important. I have something for you and Keshav. Now, can you please call your brother?"

Madhav called out to Keshav but he didn't heed as usual.

"It's for Mother, Baba ji is here and he has something for us," Madhav yelled.

Hearing this Keshav turned up. He bowed to the sage in respected and waited for him to say something.

The sage took a seed from his ragged bag and gave it to the boys.

Both the boys carefully looked at it. It was big and brown in colour. They had never seen such a seed before.

"Sow this seed in your garden. Soon the plant will grow and bear fruits that will aid your mother. The more you take care of the plant, the sooner the plant will grow but...," after a pause, the sage added, "Remember this must remain secret! You both must sow it together, water it together, and protect it together. The plant's care must be taken by four hands," saying this the sage left.

Both Keshav and Madhav were worried as their mother's health was deteriorating with each passing day. The seed which the sage gave them brought some hope.

Keshav grabbed the seed and rushed to the garden.

"Together!" shouted Madhav as he ran behind Keshav. Unwillingly, Keshav stopped and waited for Madhav to come. Both sowed the seed and watered it together as asked by the sage.

Soon, a little plant grew out of the seed. Keshav and Madhav were surprised to see it grow quickly. Working together created magic for the brothers.

The brothers who once avoided each other now exchanged smiles. They not only waited for each other to water the plant but also waited to have meals together. As the plant grew, their mother's health got better. She was happy to see her children getting together nicely. She longed for this. This change in their behaviour caught everyone's attention. The people who once enjoyed the brothers fighting were puzzled to see them getting together.

Within a few weeks, the plant was ready to bear fruits. A little fruit appeared on it. Both brothers stayed day and night next to the plant to protect it as this fruit was going to heal their mother. But, one night it rained very heavily and the plant was destroyed. Keshav and Madhav tried hard to protect it but they failed. Looking at the fallen plant and the unripen fruit, they cried.

Hearing the cries, Mother got out of her bed to look for them.

"What is wrong with you both? "She asked in a weak voice. Both Keshav and Madhav were happy to see their mother walking on her own.

"Oh Mother! you can walk on your own", Madhav cheerfully said.

"It is all because of you both. Your love and care helped me recover from the sickness" she hugged her sons saying this.

Within a few days, Mother got as healthy and active as she was before.

One day, while Keshav and Madhav were wandering in the forest for firewood, they again saw the sage meditating under the same tree. They went closer to him.

The sage noticed them and opened his eyes. The brothers bowed in respect.

"Hope your mother is doing better now", enquired the sage.

"Baba ji, she is healthy now. We are grateful to you," replied Keshav

"But we could not feed her the fruit. The plant was destroyed in the rain. We couldn't protect it. Will her illness arise later?" Madhav queried worriedly.

"Her illness has vanished. Your togetherness has brought peace and serenity to your house. She is happy that you are both caring and loving each other. Her worries turned to dust, and so did her illness." Saying this, the sage again closed his eyes and went into meditation.

The brothers understood the message and always stayed together.

www.ingramcontent.com/pod-product-compliance
Lightning Source LLC
Chambersburg PA
CBHW020503160726
47991CB00007B/2781